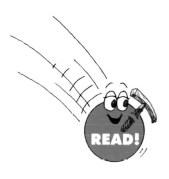

# DWIGHT AND
# THE TRILOBITE

*All inquiries should be addressed to:*
Barron's Educational Series, Inc.
250 Wireless Boulevard
Hauppauge, NY 11788

International Standard Book Number 0-8120-1839-7

Library of Congress Catalog Card Number 93-41478

**Library of Congress Cataloging-in-Publication Data**

Foster, Kelli C.
    Dwight and the trilobite / by Foster & Erickson : illustrations by
Kerri Gifford.
        p. cm.— (Get ready—get set—read!)
        Summary: Dwight and his mother Mrs. Knight go hunting for
trilobites.
        ISBN 0-8120-1839-7
        (1. Trilobites—Fiction. 2. Stories in rhyme.) I. Erickson,
Gina Clegg. II. Gifford, Kerri, ill. III. Title. IV. Series:
Erickson, Gina Clegg. Get ready—get set—read!
PZ8.3.F813Dw    1994
(E)—dc20                                                    93-41478
                                                                CIP
                                                                AC


PRINTED IN HONG KONG
4567    9927    9876543

GET READY...GET SET...READ!

# DWIGHT AND THE TRILOBITE

**by**
Foster & Erickson

**Illustrations by**
Kerri Gifford

**BARRON'S**

"Let's go find a trilobite,"
said Mrs. Knight.
"All right!" said Dwight.

"But what is a trilobite?"

"Mom, does a trilobite
try to bite?"

"No, a trilobite
does not fight."

"Are they downright fast?
Do they fly like a kite?"

"Not quite. They do not go.
They do not take flight."

"Are trilobites black,
brown, or white?"

"They might be all,"
said Mrs. Knight.

"Are they out at night
or when it's light?"

"Trilobites are out
in daylight and night."

"Is a trilobite big?"

"Stop, Dwight.
Hold this tight.
Here is a trilobite."

"But Mom, it's just a rock.
It is not alive," said Dwight.

"You are quite right,"
said Mrs. Knight.
"A trilobite is a fossil."

"Trilobites lived long ago.
This is all that's left, you know."

# THE END

# The IGHT Word Family

daylight
downright
Dwight
fight
flight
Knight
night
right
tight

# The ITE Word Family

bite
quite
trilobite
white

## Sight Words

fly
Mrs.
out
try
does
hold
know
alive
brown
lived
you're
fossil

## Dear Parents and Educators:

Welcome to *Get Ready...Get Set...Read!*

We've created these books to introduce children to the magic of reading.

Each story in the series is built around one or two word families. For example, *A Mop for Pop* uses the OP word family. Letters and letter blends are added to OP to form words such as TOP, LOP, and STOP. As you can see, once children are able to read OP, it is a simple task for them to read the entire word family. In addition to word families, we have used a limited number of "sight words." These are words found to occur with high frequency in the books your child will soon be reading. Being able to identify sight words greatly increaes reading skill.

You might find the steps outlined on the facing page useful in guiding your work with your begining reader.

We had great fun creating these books, and great pleasure sharing them with our children. We hope *Get Ready...Get Set...Read!* helps make this first step in reading fun for you and your new reader.

Kelli C. Foster, Ph.D.
Educational Psychologist

Gina Clegg Erickson, MA
Reading Specialist

# Guidelines for Using *Get Ready...Get Set...Read!*

Step 1.     Read the story to your child.

Step 2.     Have your child read the Word Family list aloud several times.

Step 3.     Invent new words for the list. Print each new combination for your child to read. Remember, nonsense words can be used (*dat, kat, gaf*).

Step 4.     Read the story *with* your child. He or she reads all of the Word Family words; you read the rest.

Step 5.     Have your child read the Sight Word list aloud several times.

Step 6.     Read the story *with* your child again. This time he or she reads the words from both lists; you read the rest.

Step 7.     Your child reads the entire book to you!

Titles in the

Series

## SET 1

Find Nat
The Sled Surprise
Sometimes I Wish
A Mop for Pop
The Bug Club
**BRING-IT-ALL-TOGETHER BOOKS**
What a Day for Flying!
Bat's Surprise

## SET 2

The Tan Can
The Best Pets Yet
Pip and Kip
Frog Knows Best
Bub and Chub
**BRING-IT-ALL-TOGETHER BOOKS**
Where Is the Treasure?
What a Trip!

## SET 3

Jake and the Snake
Jeepers Creepers
Two Fine Swine
What Rose Doesn't Know
Pink and Blue
**BRING-IT-ALL-TOGETHER BOOKS**
The Pancake Day
Hide and Seek

## SET 4

Whiptail of Blackshale Trail
Colleen and the Bean
Dwight and the Trilobite
The Old Man at the Moat
By the Light of the Moon
**BRING-IT-ALL-TOGETHER BOOKS**
Night Light
The Crossing

## SET 5

Tall and Small
Bounder's Sound
How to Catch a Butterfly
Ludlow Grows Up
Matthew's Brew
**BRING-IT-ALL-TOGETHER BOOKS**
Snow in July
Let's Play Ball

349